So What if it's Raining!

by Miriam Young
pictures by Carol Nicklaus

Parents' Magazine Press·New York

Library of Congress Cataloging in Publication Data
Young, Miriam Burt.
    So what if it's raining!
    SUMMARY: A small boy and girl have fun using their imaginations
on a rainy day.
    [1. Play—Fiction] I. Nicklaus, Carol.
II. Title.
PZ7.Y873So   [E]   75-19340
ISBN 0-8193-0803-X   ISBN 0-8193-0804-8 lib. bdg.

So What if it's Raining!

"So what if it's raining!" Jason said
to Jennifer one showery day. "We can still have fun.

"We'll pretend it has been raining for weeks and there's a

terrible flood. We have to row around rescuing people.

"Look! See that roof sticking out of the water?

There's a little spotted dog caught up there. I'd better
go and rescue him."

Jennifer liked rowing, but she didn't like Jason to
have all the fun rescuing that dog. She had once seen
a little spotted dog in the circus.

"I know what!" she said. "Let's play circus clowns now.
I'll drag in this heavy rope, and everyone will think there
must be an elephant at the other end.

"But, instead, there's a tiny dog. The audience will laugh. You'll be a fat clown in a suit stuffed out with balloons and get tangled in my rope.

"I'll wear a hat with a sign that pops up saying
OUT TO LUNCH. Then I'll pull a string of hot dogs
out of my pocket. Only they'll turn out to be
firecrackers and go off—bang! bang! bang!"

Jason liked playing circus, but he wanted to be the
one with the hot dogs. He loved going bang! bang! bang!
"I know what," he said. "Let's play Wild West.

"I'm an outlaw and you're the sheriff. We're having a shoot-out. Bang! bang! bang!

"You win and throw me in jail. But I'll just wait till you fall asleep; then I'll reach through the bars with my giant magnet and get the keys out of your pocket."

Jennifer liked playing Wild West. She liked being the sheriff, too. "Okay, only I won't really be asleep," she said. "I'll just pretend.

"And when you get outside, I'll jump up and snap the handcuffs on you.

"Then I'll ride away to my friend's ranch on YOUR horse.
So there!"

Jason didn't like the idea of Jennifer's galloping
off on his horse. "Let's both be cowboys riding
the range," he said.

"We'll have beautiful horses. Brown horses that
are twins."
Jennifer liked that idea. They rode and rode.

But after a while, Jennifer grew tired of riding. Jason looked as if he could go on bouncing and jouncing forever.

"Oh-oh! One of my stirrups is loose. It's falling
right off the saddle," said Jennifer. "I'd better hop off."
"I know how to fix leather," Jason offered hopefully.

"How come you know so much, Smarty?" snapped Jennifer.
"Because my uncle is a shoemaker and he once showed me.
That's how!"
"I know what would really be fun," Jennifer said.

"Let's play elves. There's a poor old shoemaker who has hundreds of shoes to fix. And if they're not all mended by morning, he'll be thrown into the dungeon. He works and works. But he gets so tired that he falls asleep.

"Then we sneak in, two little elves, and we mend all those shoes while he's snoring."

"Neat," said Jason. He went through the closets gathering up shoes—his mother's, his father's, his older sister's and even his grandmother's. He piled

them all on the floor, and then he and Jennifer sat down to work.

After a while Jason began to feel hungry. "Well, we've finished the last shoe. Let's go before the shoemaker wakes up. Maybe we can find some cookies."

They went out to the kitchen and looked in the cabinets, but all they found were plain crackers. "What I'd like is chocolate-chip cookies," Jason said. "I wonder if we have any chocolate chips? Maybe Grandma would help us make some. Or how about fudge?"

"There's only one problem," said Jennifer. "If I eat fudge,
I'm supposed to brush my teeth right afterwards so
I won't get cavities. And that takes the good taste away.
You know what would be great? Fudge-flavored
toothpaste that keeps you from getting cavities!"

"Let's invent some!" said Jason. "Let's be scientists
who invent all sorts of great things. Fudge toothpaste.
Vitamin cookies. A robot that cleans your room.
A computer to write thank-you letters to aunts. A clock
that makes time go slowly when you're having fun…"

Time! Jennifer looked at the kitchen clock. It was nearly five o'clock. "Pooh," she said. "I've got to go home. Just when we were having such a good time. And tomorrow it's supposed to be sunny. We'll have to play outside."

"So WHAT if it's sunny!" said Jason. "Come on over.
We can still have fun."

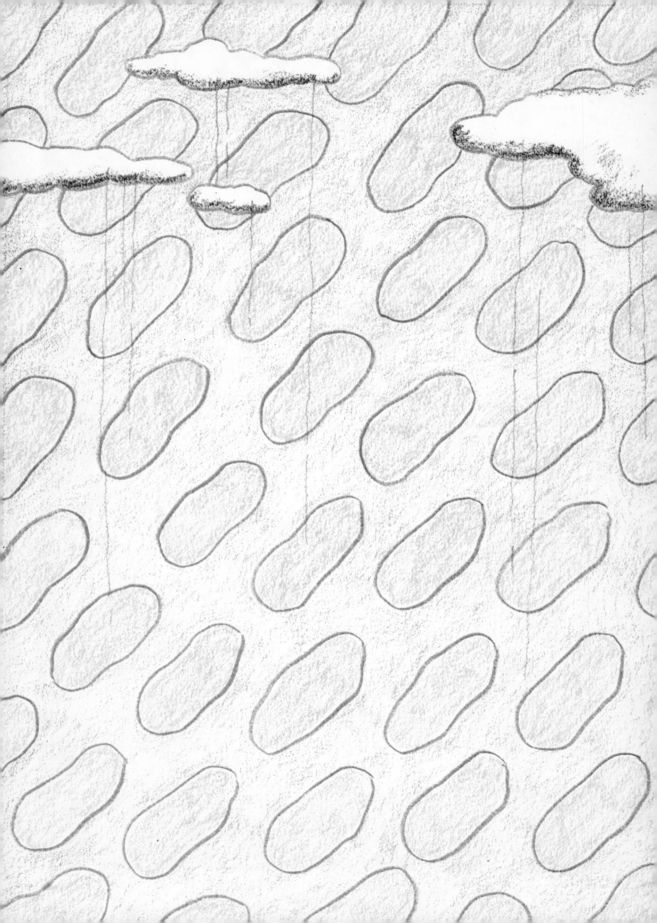